A IS FOR **ART**

AN ABSTRACT ALPHABET

STEPHEN T. JOHNSON

A Paula Wiseman Book
Simon & Schuster Books for Young Readers
New York London Toronto Sydney

SIMON & SCHUSTER BOOKS FOR YOUNG READERS
An imprint of Simon & Schuster Children's Publishing Division
1230 Avenue of the Americas, New York, New York 10020
Copyright © 2008 by Stephen T. Johnson
All rights reserved, including the right of reproduction in whole or in part in any form.
SIMON & SCHUSTER BOOKS FOR YOUNG READERS is a trademark of Simon & Schuster, Inc.
Book design by Stephen T. Johnson
The text for this book is set in Minion.
Manufactured in the United States of America
2 4 6 8 10 9 7 5 3
Library of Congress Cataloging-in-Publication Data
Johnson, Stephen T., 1964–
A is for art : an abstract alphabet / Stephen T. Johnson.
p. cm.
"A Paula Wiseman book."
ISBN-13: 978-0-689-86301-1 (hardcover)
ISBN-10: 0-689-86301-2 (hardcover)
1. Art, Abstract—Juvenile literature. 2. English language—Alphabet—Juvenile literature.
[1. Alphabet—Juvenile literature.] I. Title.
N6494.A2.J64 2008
709.2—dc22
2007030224

Front and back case covers: Details from *Variations on a Vertical*

AUTHOR'S NOTE

When I was growing up in the Midwest, two pieces of original art hung on the walls in my bedroom. One was a beautiful charcoal portrait of an elderly man, drawn by my grandfather, J. Theodore Johnson, while an art student at the Art Institute of Chicago. The other was a watercolor I had painted when I was three years old, titled *Elephant,* according to my mother's handwriting on the back. These two works are examples of contrasting modes of visual expression—specifically realism and abstraction—that have informed my development as an artist.

The precise yet subtle use of charcoal in my grandfather's portrait, built layer after layer, stroke after stroke, is still marvelous to behold. Indeed, my passion for drawing and painting while in art school at the University of Kansas was fueled by my desire to draw like him. Yet I always felt an affinity for my little watercolor for its bold use of color and adventurous use of the medium. Today in my own children's drawings and paintings I see this same sense of creativity and freedom.

J. Theodore Johnson (1902–1963)
Portrait of a Man, ca. 1923
Charcoal on paper
24 7/8 x 18 3/4 inches

Over the years my affinity for nineteenth- and early-twentieth-century art lessened and my interest in modern and contemporary art, particularly abstract expressionism, conceptual art, Dadaism and neo-Dadaism, new realism, pop art, and postminimalism flourished. Having created a successful art career with realistic drawings and paintings in the late 1980s and '90s, I found myself returning to my little watercolor *Elephant* hanging on the wall of my studio in New York City. I wanted to move out of what I perceived to be the confines of realism to explore the more open, expansive, and experimental possibilities inherent in abstraction.

The paintings, collages, installations, sculptures, and multiples in this book, *A Is for Art: An Abstract Alphabet*, are a direct result of this desire. They invite viewers to think about and question art as children do, asking: What is art? What are the ideas behind a work of art? Do they work? Why or why not? Who decides what is art? Can anything be used to make art? And so on.

Through hundreds of presentations in schools and libraries on the process of creating children's books, particularly my use of the alphabet as a source of inspiration since the publication of my first alphabet book in 1995, I have seen firsthand the wonderment and pleasure that children have when they see the world differently. Their questions, thoughts, and irrepressible enthusiasm about how one transforms an idea into something visual and real, and watching how they make instant connections in their minds, inevitably astounds me.

Stephen T. Johnson
Elephant, 1967
Watercolor on paper
8 3/8 x 10 7/8 inches

For the past six years I have been exploring the English dictionary, selectively choosing and organizing particular words from each letter of the alphabet and, based solely on the meanings of the words, developing a visual work of art. I took ordinary objects and made them unfamiliar, removing functionality in order to reveal their potential metaphorical associations, which can lead in turn to overlapping and sometimes paradoxical meanings. I call these individual works "literal abstractions" and the ongoing series An Abstract Alphabet.

The self-imposed limitations and restrictive nature of using only words from each letter of the alphabet to generate an original creation have turned out to be enormously liberating. And so, I have sought to expand upon artist Marcel Duchamp's concept of the "ready-made," Robert Rauschenberg's playful curiosity with new materials, and Jeff Koons's *modus operandi* of art as readily accessible. And just for fun, I have included the letter shapes of each letter of the alphabet in all the works. Well, most anyway—you'll see.

For me, art, like language, is about discovery. At its very best it can be moving, transcendent. Or on a visceral level it can simply make one laugh out loud. Art provokes, confounds, challenges, surprises, informs, rejuvenates, and stretches our way of seeing the world. We cannot get enough of it. So I hope that my work in this book will ignite and inspire dialogues about art, words, and ideas, which might quicken children and adults to generate creative associations and explore new ways of pulling abstractions out of the real.

—Stephen T. Johnson

AN ABSTRACT ALPHABET

A a

Arrangement No. 1

Affixed across and around an angled letter *A* are an array of abstracted and assembled bits of advertisements, and apparent among them are apostrophes, ampersands, accents, and an asterisk.

Bb

Blueberry Blues

Beside a bisected, black, bumpy bicycle tire, a bunch of busy burgundy brushstrokes blurs into a blue background with a broken bowl below at the bottom.

Camouflage
Countless colorful candies consciously collected, crammed, crushed, and confined crowd a clear circular container filled to capacity.

Dd

Dotty Diptych
Densely distributed dominoes, divided by dark and light dots on dual panels, disappear under drips of dramatically dashed paint dribbling downwards.

 **E e**

Evidence
Examining the enigmatic elements in this work exposes an eagle, an ear, an elongated English red earthworm, an egg and dart motif (upper right edge), the Eiffel Tower, and an exclamation point!

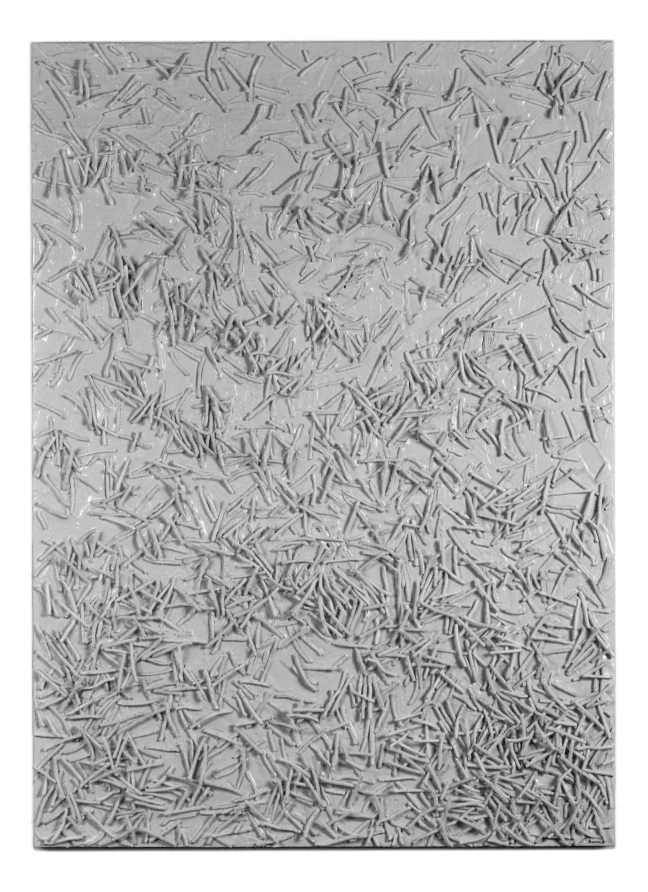

Ff

Fast Food Frenzy

Fourteen hundred and fifty-five fake French fries were flipped, flicked, and flung onto a full-size field of faint fuchsia.

(Find the letter *F* in *Evidence* on the facing page.)

Gg

Golden Sections
Gradations of green, gray, and gold geometric groupings rendered with gouache, graphite, glitter, granulated gunpowder, and glue generate glimpses into golden ratios and the gamut of Greek thought.

Hh

Hoopla!
Hordes of handmade, homogeneously hued, hollow hula hoops in a huge heap hang and hover from a hook high up, where the letter *H* is hidden.

I i

Ice Cream Floats

Indoors, in an industrial interior, is an installation of individually illuminated, isolated, immobilized, immersed, inverted, identical, insoluble imitation ice cream cones.

Jj

Jambalaya
Jampacked juxtapositions of jagged, jutting, jammed, and jumbled junk joyfully and judiciously joined.

Kk

Keepsake
Knitted kitchen cloth, key, keyholes, kapok, knots, and knobs keep company near a king's blue stripe on a king-size, kelly green canvas.

L l

Landscape
Latched to the left of a long, long painting layered with lemon
yellow, lavender, and light red latex and lit by a little lightbulb, a
lime green ladder leans.

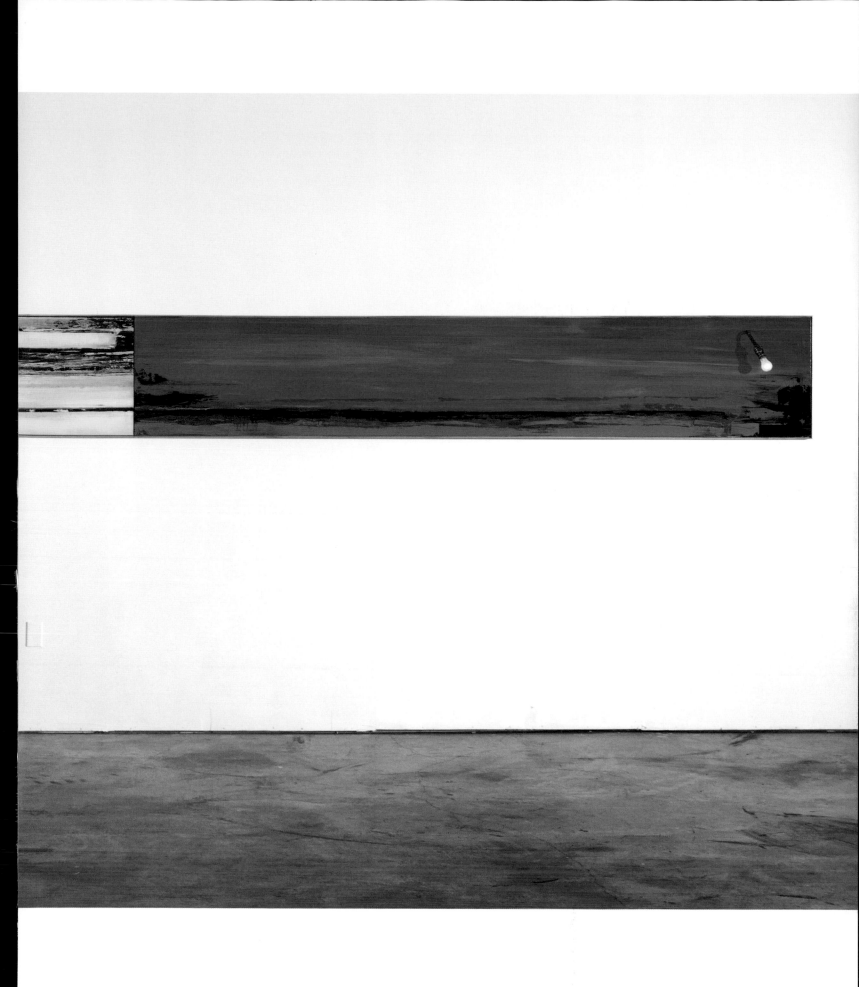

M m

Meditation on the Memory of a Princess
Motionless, a man-made, monochromatic magenta mass mimics multiple mattresses and makes a massive mound near a mini mauve marble.

(Look for the missing letter *M* in the letter *R*.)

Nn

Nocturne
Number nineteen is next to the letter *N*; nearby, the number nine neighbors a Naples yellow number ninety-nine.

Oo

Object

Offset on an overall opaque orange oval is one off-centered, off-white oblique.

(The omitted letter *O* occupies the upper left on the opposite page.)

Pop Quiz

Packed into this panoramic picture are: Pancakes. Potato chips. Pencils. Pale pink paper clips. Photo-realistic peas. Peanuts. Popcorn. A pinwheel. A plug. A plastic peeing putto. A portrait of a parrot in profile. A pen point. Polka-dots. Peacock feathers. Puzzle pieces. Purple paint pouring, pouring . . . period!

Qq

Quiet Time Quilt
Queen-size quilt quartered by quadrants, with quadrilaterals,
quotation marks, and question marks, invites queries as to
queens, quilts, and quietude.

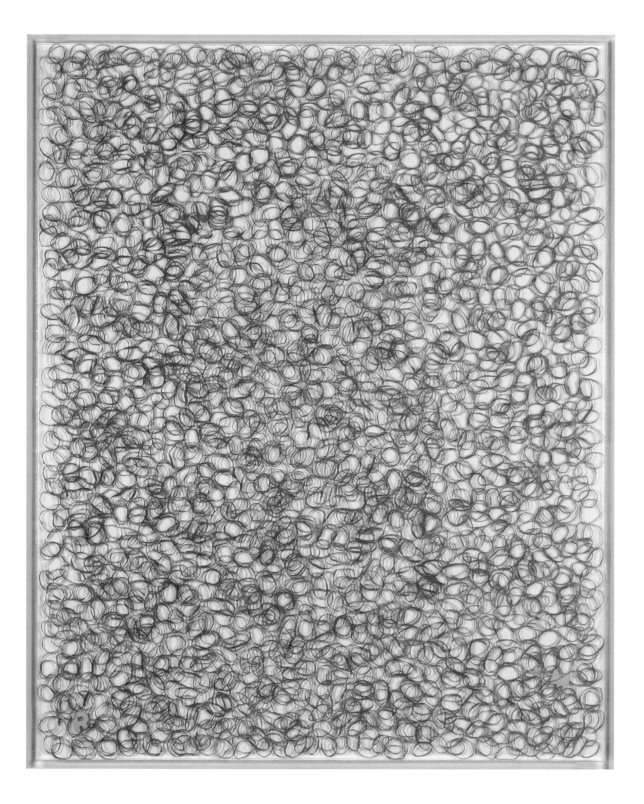

Rr

Recycled

Randomly placed, ready-made red and blue round rubber bands, rendered rigid by resin, reside in an upright rectangular receptacle.

(Remember to look for the missing letter *M*.)

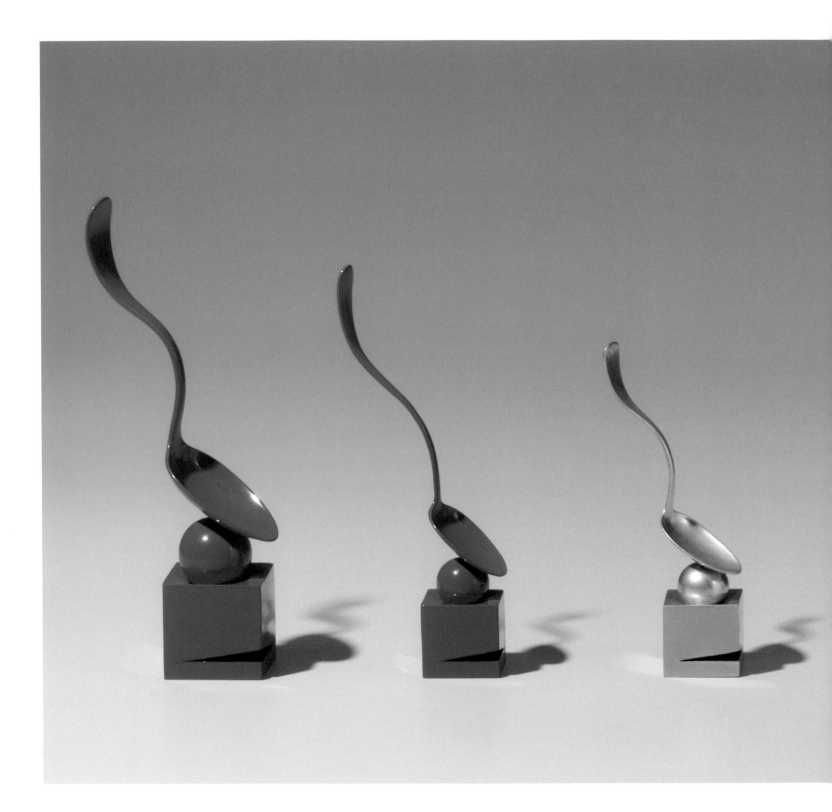

S s

Souvenir Series
Several sizes of shiny, solid, spoon-shaped, semiabstract sanguine, silver, and slate black sculptural statuettes standing on similar sleek-surfaced spheres, sunken in simple square stands with slits, cast soft, svelte, sinuous shadows.

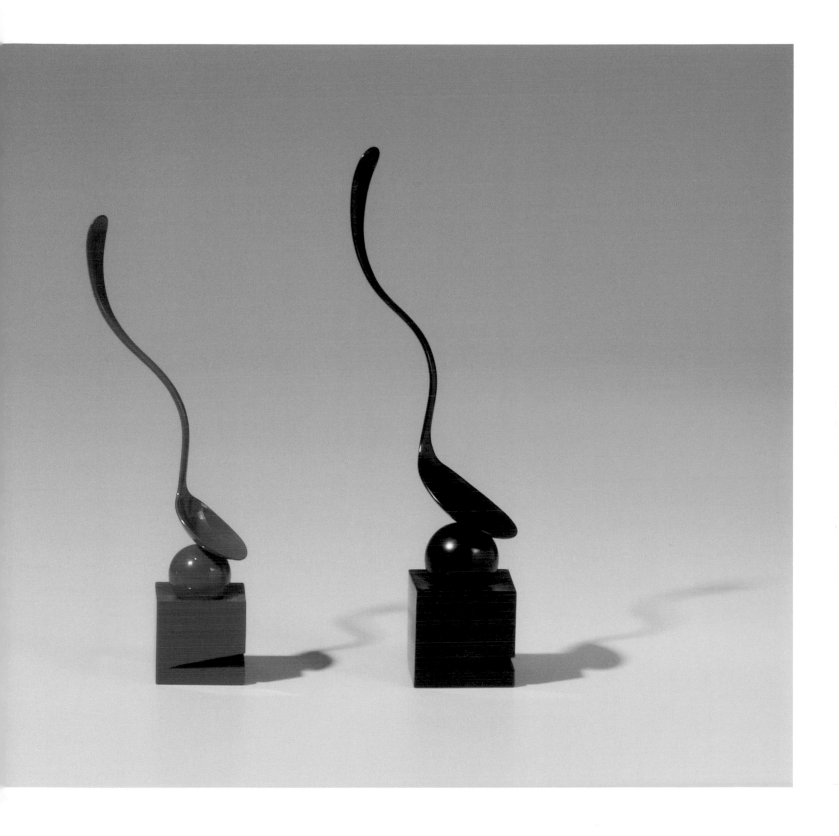

T t

Triptych

Thick-textured titanium white paint. Torn tan tape. Tabs. Triangles. Thin transparent tracing paper. A tag. Two-dimensional typewritten text. Three tarnished thumbtacks. Ten teal blue thumbprints. A tilted *T*. A tiny three-dimensional toy to tease out trains of thought.

U u

Untitled
Underneath—an umber-colored circle. Upside—uneven,
unequal, ultramarine blue undulates around an upside-down,
underlined, uppercase, umlauted *U*.

Variations on a Vertical
Violet vents? Vibrantly vivid vermicelli? Vanishing vowels on verdant vinyl? A visually vertiginous vocalise?

Ww

Wrapped Wishes
White waxy wall hangings, wrinkled and wavy—
one wonders what's within.

XXI Century Song
X-rays and xerographs of xylophones examine experiences
exactly, expertly, exquisitely.

Yy

Yum Yum
Yams and yellow yolk on a yo-yo with yellow ochre-colored yarn.
Yes!

Zz

Zippy
Zigging and zagging through a zodiac, zinnia, and zebra zips a zigzag.

Index of the sizes, materials, and location of letters

Boxes show where the letters are  hidden.

Arrangement No. 1
collage mounted on canvas
19 1/2 x 10 inches
49.1 x 25.4 cm

Blueberry Blues
oil, enamel, bicycle tire, bowl,
and collage on canvas
78 x 68 inches
198.1 x 172.7 cm

Camouflage
Plexiglas and commercially
confected candies
48 inches diameter x 3 inches deep
121.9 cm diameter x 7.6 cm deep

Dotty Diptych
dominoes, oil, and enamel
paint on two wooden panels
80 x 72 inches
203.2 x 182.9 cm

Evidence
oil, ink, house paint, graphite,
and collage on wood
21 x 24 inches
53.3 x 61 cm

Fast Food Frenzy
fake French fries and acrylic
paint on wooden panel
75 x 54 inches (full size)
190.5 x 137.2 cm

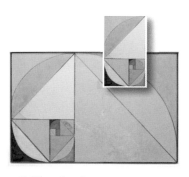

Golden Sections
gouache, graphite, glitter,
gunpowder, gesso, glassine, and
collage on paper mounted on panel
26 1/2 x 40 1/2 inches
67.3 x 102.9 cm

Hoopla!
painted aluminum, steel
wire rope, and hook
14 x 5 x 5 feet
426.7 x 152.4 x 152.4 cm

Ice Cream Floats
resin, monofilament, mirror,
reverse osmosis water, iodine,
tracing dye, lights, powder-coated
steel, painted wooden bases, and
electrical components
64 x 12 1/2 x 12 1/2 inches each
162.6 x 31.8 x 31.8 cm each

Jambalaya
steel, aluminum, vinyl,
rubber, and plastics
19 x 13 x 6 inches
48.3 x 33 x 15.2 cm

Keepsake
oil, key, kapok, wooden
knobs, and twine on canvas
80 x 76 inches (king size)
203.2 x 193 cm

Landscape
oil and latex enamel on two
wooden panels, with illuminated
electric light, lightbulb, and
wooden ladder
18 x 228 inches (24 ft)
45.7 x 579.1 cm

Meditation on the Memory of a Princess

Nazdar printer's ink, vinyl-coated nylon, molded plastic, nylon cording, 110-volt internal blower fan, and extension cord
108 x 108 x 144 inches
(9 x 9 x 12 ft)
274.3 x 274.3 x 365.8 cm
glass marble
1 x 1 inches
2.5 x 2.5 cm

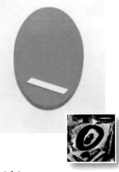

Nocturne

oil, ink, gouache, charcoal, pastel, and collage on paper mounted to canvas
25 x 24 inches
63.5 x 61 cm

Object

oil and collage on wooden table
34 x 22 x 16 inches
86.4 x 55.9 x 40.6 cm

Pop Quiz

(a preparatory piece for a painting)
collage on paper
11 1/2 x 29 inches
29.2 x 73.6 cm

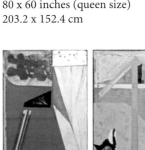

Quiet Time Quilt

quilted cotton fabric
80 x 60 inches (queen size)
203.2 x 152.4 cm

Recycled

rubber bands, epoxy resin, wooden puzzle pieces, and Plexiglas
64 x 51 x 2 1/2 inches
162.6 x 129.5 x 6.4 cm

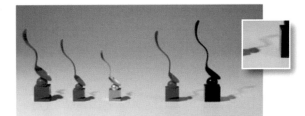

Souvenir Series

powder-coated steel, various sizes from
6 1/4 x 3 x 1 1/2 inches
to 10 x 3 x 2 inches
15.9 x 7.6 x 3.8 cm
to 25.4 x 7.6 x 5.1 cm

Triptych

oil, gouache, collage, tape, thumbtacks, tracing paper, and wooden train on three wooden panels
28 1/2 x 55 1/2 inches
72.4 x 141 cm

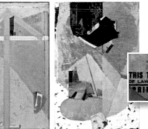

Untitled

oil on shaped wood
54 x 54 x 5 inches
137.2 x 137.2 x 12.7 cm

Variations on a Vertical

oil, enamel, vinyl, metal vents, and collage on aluminum panels
87 x 36 inches
221 x 91.4 cm

Wrapped Wishes

wax, wool, objects, and wire, various sizes, from
12 x 16 inches to 29 x 22 inches
30.5 x 40.6 to 73.7 x 55.9 cm

XXI Century Song

xanthene yellow dye, X-rays, and xerography collage, painted metal box, lights, electrical components, and wire
26 x 22 x 3 inches
(including frame)
66 x 55.9 x 7.6 cm

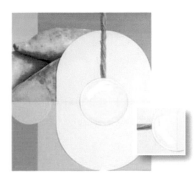

Yum Yum

oil, enamel, pastel, fabric, photographic reproductions, and collage on canvas
73 x 64 inches
185.4 x 162.6 cm

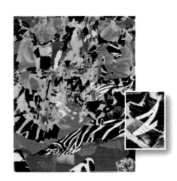

Zippy

oil, enamel, ink, pastel, crayons, charcoal, Zipatone, and collage on canvas
63 1/2 x 49 inches
161.3 x 124.5 cm

ACKNOWLEDGMENTS

A Is for Art: An Abstract Alphabet would not be a book without the unflagging enthusiasm and support provided by my editor, Paula Wiseman, during the many years that I took to complete the final works. The challenges I encountered by working with new and unusual materials, and the scale and structural complexities involved, as well as the substantial fabrication costs that ensued, slowed me down considerably and caused repeated delays in the publication of the book. Paula's patience and grace throughout were exemplary.

I would also like to express my gratitude and heartfelt thanks to my publisher, Rubin Pfeffer, and to the wonderful production and design departments at Simon & Schuster for their spirited engagement, care, and attention to every aspect in producing this stunning book.

In order to bring to fruition several of the works reproduced in *A Is for Art: An Abstract Alphabet*, I engaged those whose exceptional craft and knowledge would help me to create works of art of the highest quality. I like to say that it takes a village to make an art show, and in this case the village was Lawrence, Kansas, rich with talent and creativity. Everyone listed is from this and neighboring communities except where mentioned.

I am deeply indebted to my friend and colleague Cotter Mitchell, whose ability to shape aluminum, plastic, Plexiglas, steel, and wood was invaluable. His remarkable generosity of time, skill, and creative problem solving was critical in making many of my visions a reality. I am also extremely grateful to photographer Jon Blumb for his outstanding camera work and his methodical attention to every detail as evident in the beautiful set of images in this book.

My profound thanks extend to quilter Pamela P. Mayfield, who stitched my quilt to perfection, and to sculptors Jim Brothers and Kathy Correll, along with Elizabeth Hatchett, for their time, insight, and expertise in connection with the casting of my ice cream cones. In addition, I am very grateful to Michael Hager, professor of sculpture at Washburn University, for his help in procuring and casting resin and to the Washburn Art Department for the extended use of their terrific sculpture facilities.

I would like to recognize and thank the following people and businesses for the various services and goods they provided in conjunction with creating the artwork: percussionist Kevin Bobo and the Music Department at the University of Kansas; Larry Brow; John Conard; Custom Coatings and Metal, LLC; Chris Wolfe Edmonds; Electric Supply Lighting, Inc.; Gria, Inc.; Dave Hamill; Linda James; Ted and Mary Johnson; Jeff Hutchison and Marty Kennedy of Kennedy Glass, Inc.; Justin Kogl; the Lawrence Art Center; Dr. Jim Mandigo, head of radiology at Lawrence Memorial Hospital; Sarah's Fabrics; Todd Rogers; Bob Werts of Waxman Candles; Stephen Woods; and the many talented people at Aerostar International in Sioux Falls, South Dakota, who worked patiently with me on my designs and redesigns, beautifully incorporating the custom-made side vents and button tops into my mattress piece.

Finally, I wish to express a very special thank-you to my agent, Amy Berkower of Writers House, Inc. in New York City, and to director Saralyn Reece Hardy and her entire staff at the Spencer Museum of Art.